BABY SISTER S

BY
MERCER MAYER

A GOLDEN BOOK • NEW YORK

Western Publishing Company, Inc., Racine, Wisconsin 53404

Library of Congress Catalog Card Number: 86-82368
ISBN: 0-307-11949-1 / ISBN: 0-307-61949-4 (lib. bdg.)   MCMXCIII

My baby sister
always says no.

One day my friend
came over to play.
But my baby sister
wouldn't leave us alone.

We started to make a model boat,
but my baby sister said,

We wanted to make a blanket tent,
but my baby sister said,
"NO BLANKET!"

I tried to give her one of her dolls,
but she wasn't interested. She said,
"NO DOLL!"

"Let's play our favorite board game," my friend said.
But my baby sister said,

We went into my room
and shut the door.
But my sister said,
"NO SHUT!"

Then Mom made me open the door.

We ran outside, but my sister said,
"NO RUN!" and followed us.

I sat on my swing, but my sister said,

We tried to play ball, but my sister said,
"NO BALL!"

I thought if I sat on her bike,
she might forget about the ball.
But she didn't care. She said,
"NO BIKE...BALL!" and she
carried it off.

We didn't want to play with her tricycle, anyway.
So we came back inside to play cards.

But my sister said,
"NO CARDS, NO CARDS!"

So I got out my favorite cars and trucks.
But guess who said,
"NO CARS, NO TRUCKS!"

We decided to watch cartoons instead,
but my sister said,
"NO 'TOONS!"

So I yelled,
"MAMA!"

Then Mama said, "NAP!"
But my sister said,

But Mama always wins, and my sister took a nap.